T0368429

The Wishing Star

Written by Teresa C. Sinchak
Illustrations by Vince Dorse

Balboa Press books may be ordered through booksellers or by contacting:

Balboa Press
A Division of Hay House
1663 Liberty Drive
Bloomington, IN 47403
www.balboapress.com
844-682-1282

Because of the dynamic nature of the Internet, any web addresses or links contained in this book may have changed since publication and may no longer be valid. The views expressed in this work are solely those of the author and do not necessarily reflect the views of the publisher, and the publisher hereby disclaims any responsibility for them.

Any people depicted in stock imagery provided by Getty Images are models, and such images are being used for illustrative purposes only.
Certain stock imagery © Getty Images.

The news media has presented many stories of individuals using visualization and positive thinking to overcome or at least help with physical and/or emotional challenges. However, the characters and story of this book are fictional and any resemblance to actual persons, living or deceased or actual events is purely coincidental.

The content of this book is in no way intended to substitute the advice of a medical professional. Always consult your physician for your individual needs. The author and publisher disclaim any liability in connection with the use of this book's content. This book is for informational purposes only and the use of this book implies your acceptance of this disclaimer.

Interior Image Credit: Vince Dorse

ISBN: 979-8-7652-5055-6 (sc)
979-8-7652-5056-3 (e)

Print information available on the last page.

Balboa Press rev. date: 04/05/2024

This story

is meant to inspire

everyone who reads these pages

and to dare to stretch

the limits of their

Imagination.

To my Parents, Stanley and Mary Sinchak,

Thank You for teaching me to Believe

and for your Love that gave me insight to

the Beauty and Goodness

in Everything.

" ... *remember, your thoughts create your future*".

In the town of Clearview lived a girl named Sarah. From a young age Sarah displayed an unusual imagination that she shared with just about

anyone . . . like the mailman, "Would you like to meet
my friends?" she asked . . . or her neighbor, Mr. Adams.
"Hey, look at that dog!" she shouted, pointing to the clouds.

But as Sarah grew older her imagination sometimes got her into trouble . . .
like the time she imagined flying with birds and missed her school bus . . .

. . . or the time she told her teacher about aliens landing in her back yard. "Oh, really?" Mrs. Cabbagestalk replied.

It wasn't long before her parents sat her down for a serious talk. "Sarah," her father began,"you're mother and I are concerned that your imagination is getting out of hand. You're older now and it's time to stop imagining."

So, to stay out of trouble, Sarah kept busy with other activities. She chased butterflies, collected bugs and searched for bird's nests. One day Sarah spotted a large nest in the old oak tree. "Hm", she thought, "I wonder how many eggs are up there?" Sarah climbed the tree until the nest was within reach . . .

. . . but as she leaned over to grab a branch, she
lost her balance and came tumbling to the ground.

For several weeks Sarah was in the hospital recovering from her accident. She was examined by the very best doctors and given the very best treatment . . . but Sarah couldn't walk. Dr. Smith reported to her parents, "I'm sorry, Mr. and Mrs. Rogers, we did everything we could." When Sarah returned home she tried to keep busy in bed. However, each day she grew more restless.

Then one night while looking out her window Sarah noticed
an unusual star. "Could this be a wishing star?" she wondered.

At that moment Sarah felt goose bumps. "Oooooh", she whispered.
This wasn't an ordinary star. Taking a deep breath, Sarah made a wish!

The wishing star reminded Sarah of her grandfather. She remembered
him tell her how they brought hope to those who believed. On clear

summer nights he would point his telescope to the sky and name all
the stars. "Look over there, Sarah," she remembered him say, "that's
the North Star". Sarah missed him very much since he passed away.
From his hospital bed she recalled his last words to her. "Sarah, dear,
time goes by so quickly . . . make the most of your life . . .

. . . remember, your thoughts create your future."

The next few days Sarah thought about her grandfather's words.
Finally, she heard his voice inside her say, "You have it in you, Sarah.
Just believe!" Sarah smiled, remembering how she always trusted
her grandfather. "I believe, grandpa," she whispered back to him.
From that moment, Sarah was determined to create her future.

First, Sarah drew pictures of her legs being well again.

Then, she imagined herself running, jumping and playing.

In her mind Sarah traveled to far away places, climbing mountains,
hiking forests, exploring jungles and snorkeling ocean waters.

Everyday Sarah imagined a new adventure. She saw all the colors bright and clear, from red sunsets to green forests, yellow butterflies and purple fish.

In her mind Sarah tasted the salty ocean water, she smelled the fresh pine trees, she heard the roar of the elephants in the jungle and she felt the hard

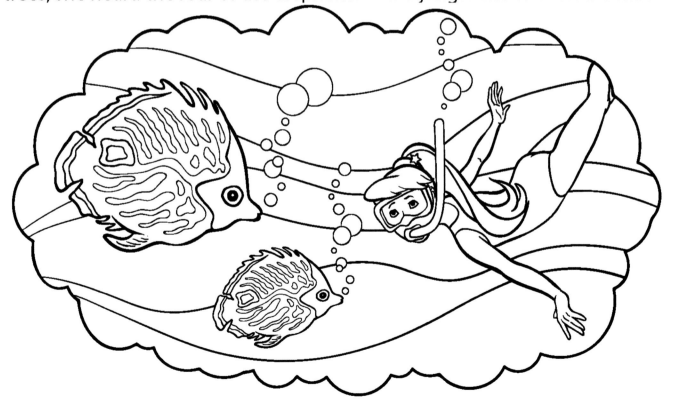

mountain rock. Sarah used her imagination to make everything real.

As the months passed Sarah continued her imaginary adventures.

Then one morning Sarah was awaken by birds chirping outside her window.

As she gave a big stretch, Sarah felt a warm tingling spread down her legs. Throwing off her covers, Sarah felt her legs move! "Wooow!" she shouted.

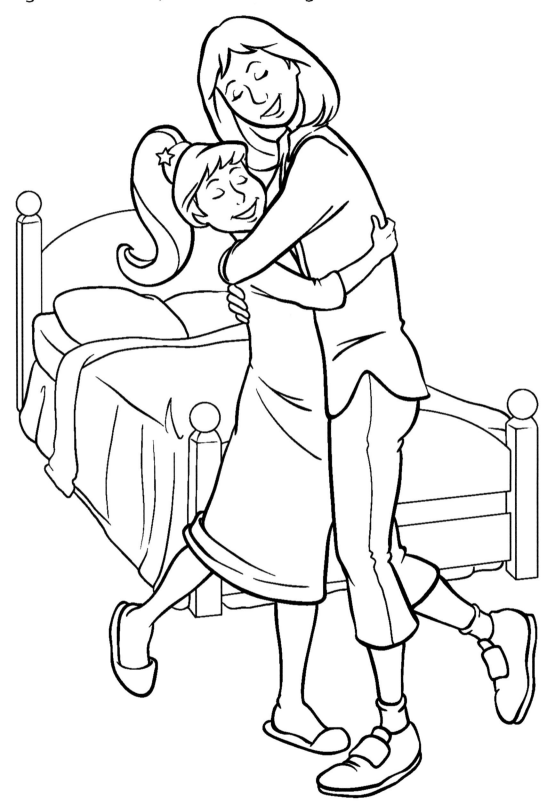

Holding her breath and lowering her feet to the floor, Sarah took a step! "Mom! Dad!" she cried. Sarah's mom rushed to her side with a big hug.

A few weeks later Sarah and her parents returned to Dr. Smith's office.

As he watched Sarah walk across the room, he scratched his head and turned to Sarah's parents, "Sometimes we see this sort of thing happen.

There's really no explanation." But Sarah knew. "There is an explanation, Dr. Smith," she assured him. "It was the wishing star and my imagination that made my legs well again!"

That summer . . .

. . . Sarah chased butterflies, collected bugs and searched for birds nests.

And every night . . .

. . . Sarah thinks of her grandfather and the wishing star.

Searching within can help find answers to many of our situations. Drawing is one way to help become aware of solutions and to develop creativity. The next few pages provide activities that can assist with finding the answers within. If you are unable to draw, use your mind to create the images. Regardless of what your drawing talent may be just know that whatever you draw is right for you.

ACTIVITY #1 IDENTIFY THE SITUATION YOU WANT CHANGED

Pick one thing in your life that you would like to change. Now draw a picture of what it looks like or how you think it might look. The first picture that comes to your mind is usually the one to go with, but if you feel that you need some time to think about how it looks that's OK too.

ACTIVITY #2   CREATE THE HELPER

Now draw a picture of something that would help make those changes that you want. One example could be a superhero, one that you are familiar with or one that you create using your own imagination. Another example might be an animal or some sort of creature, computer or anything else that you can imagine. Be creative with this and go with what feels the best for you.

ACTIVITY #3   THE MOTION PICTURE

Now draw a picture of how the Helper would change the situation. Draw the Helper doing something to the situation to make the change that you want. Have the picture show the situation already changed. Let your imagination run wild here. Make the picture funny. The more ridiculous and absurd you make the picture, the better! Draw the picture so that when you look at it you will laugh out loud. Then think about this picture as often as you can.

ACTIVITY #4   CREATE YOUR FUTURE

Make a list of activities that you like to do or would like to do. See yourself doing those activities as often as you can. Make it real by using all your five senses of sight, smell, taste, touch and hearing. Keep positive and trust yourself. Your mind can take you anywhere you want to go!

Printed in the United States
by Baker & Taylor Publisher Services